To Case[...]
from first grade. [...]
Job!

Love,
Mom & Dad

6-10-04

Winky Blue
Goes Wild!

by Pamela Jane
Illustrated by Debbie Tilley

For my good friends Gary, Robin, Sarah, and Brandon Karpf—
hurrah for the pumpkin pie!—P.J.

For Gillian—D.T.

Special thanks to my editor Don L. Curry for his good humor
and light touch—P.J.

Text copyright © 2003 by Pamela Jane
Illustrations copyright © 2003 by Debbie Tilley
under exclusive license to MONDO Publishing

For information contact:
MONDO Publishing
980 Avenue of the Americas
New York, NY 10018
Visit our web site at http://www.mondopub.com

Printed in the United States of America
03 04 05 06 07 08 09 HC 9 8 7 6 5 4 3 2 1
03 04 05 06 07 08 09 PB 9 8 7 6 5 4 3 2 1
ISBN 1-59034-588-6 (hardcover)   ISBN 1-59034-589-4 (pbk.)
Designed by Symon Chow

Library of Congress Cataloging-in-Publication Data

    Jane, Pamela.
      Winky Blue goes wild! / by Pamela Jane; illustrated by Debbie Tilley
        p. cm
      Summary: Rosie hopes she will win the American Museum of Natural History's pet
mummy contest, but the competition is disrupted when her pet parakeet Winky Blue and
her classmate's pet gerbil Cinnamon get loose in the museum.
      ISBN 1-59034-588-6 – ISBN 1-59034-589-4 (pbk.)
      [1. School field trips—Fiction. 2. Contests—Fiction. 3. Parakeets—Fiction. 4.
Gerbils—Fiction. 5. Pets—Fiction. 6. American Museum of Natural History—Fiction. 7.
Museums—Fiction. 8. New York. (N.Y.)—Fiction.] I. Tilley, Debbie, ill. II. Title.

PZ7.J213 Wk 2003
[Fic]—dc21   2002033381

Contents

Famous Forever

"I'm so excited!" Rosie exclaimed to her friends, Michael and Eliza, as they slowly walked home from school, enjoying the warm September sunshine. "Winky Blue's mummy is finally finished. It's the most magnificent parakeet mummy in the whole wide world!"

A lady watering pansies in her yard glanced up, startled, by Rosie's remark. Michael and Eliza didn't look surprised at all by the seemingly strange comment.

"I glued noodles onto Cinnamon's mummy," said Michael. "It looks kind of—different."

Hearing his name, Cinnamon, Michael's gerbil, poked his head out of Michael's backpack and sniffed the spicy autumn air.

"Mrs. Kompass likes things that are different," said Eliza. "She says that makes them special."

Mrs. Kompass, their teacher, was definitely different—and special—herself. She was the one who had come up with the idea of making pet mummies, which are mummies molded out of clay in the shape of your pet and decorated to look like the Egyptian mummies of long ago. And tomorrow, Mrs. Kompass planned to take the children, along with their real-life pets, to the pet mummy contest at the American Museum of Natural History in New York City. The top three winners would have their pet mummies placed on display at the museum.

"Raffles's mummy is in the doghouse," Eliza confided, as they turned the corner onto Lincoln Avenue. "I'm mad at it because its tail won't stay on."

Raffles was Eliza's dog, of course. He came bounding toward them as his name was

mentioned, his tail wagging wildly. (Unlike the dog mummy, Raffles's tail appeared to be firmly attached.)

Rosie thought with satisfaction of her own pet mummy, ready and waiting on her desk at home. Its wings glittered with colored sparkles and its head was crowned with a gold parakeet charm from Rosie's bracelet. The ancient Egyptians often decorated their mummies with scenes from everyday life. So on the back of her mummy, Rosie had painted a picture of Winky Blue helping to save Cinnamon from falling off the top of the Empire State Building. That wasn't exactly everyday life, but it was a moment worth remembering.

Winky Blue, Rosie's parakeet, was famous in Rosie's small town for his feats of bravery and courage. His big break had come last spring, when he won a "fly-on" part on *The Royal Rascals* TV show. Afterward, Rosie waited by the phone for a Hollywood producer to call and offer Winky a starring role in a blockbuster movie. But not a single producer called, and before long everyone forgot about Winky Blue. That was the trouble with fame—at least with parakeet fame anyway. It just didn't last.

Mrs. Kompass said that the ancient Egyptians mummified their pets because they loved them and wanted them to live forever. Rosie knew that Winky Blue would not live forever no matter how much she loved him.

But if he won the contest tomorrow, Winky and his mummy would be famous forever, and that was almost as good.

"When you study mummies, you find out about the way the Egyptians lived and thought," Rosie's teacher had explained. "It's almost as if the mummies speak to us from the past."

Rosie wasn't interested in the past. She was interested in the future.

"I can hardly wait until the contest tomorrow," said Rosie. "I have butterflies in my stomach just thinking about it!"

"Raffles is excited, too. Just look at him!" said Eliza, as Raffles went racing after a squirrel.

They had reached the second house from the corner, where Rosie lived with her Aunt Maria and Winky Blue. It was a small white house, set comfortably between Michael's blue bungalow and Eliza's mansion. (Eliza's house wasn't really a mansion, but Rosie liked to think of it that way, because it had three stories and a red brick turret on top.)

Rosie cut across her front yard, singing to herself.

"Winky Blue, Winky Blue, you'll be a star and your mummy will, too!"

"Don't forget, my mom said you and Eliza can come over after dinner and watch *The Wizard of OZ!*" Michael called after Rosie. "Watching a movie will make the time go by faster!"

Michael was right. Time did go faster watching *The Wizard of OZ*, especially because they had to fast-forward every time the wicked witch came on so Lily, Michael's little sister, wouldn't have nightmares. Somehow the witch seemed more funny than scary when she was wicked at high speed.

"If only life could be like the movies,"

thought Rosie, as she watched the witch whiz by. "I could fast-forward myself right into tomorrow morning!"

But that night, as Rosie lay in bed watching the moonlight shining through the maple tree, time seemed to stand still. Winky was asleep under his cage cover on her desk by the window. Rosie could see the silhouette of the parakeet mummy, its wings outstretched in the silvery light. She remembered what Mrs. Kompass had said about mummies being able to speak from the past.

Lying in the dark, thinking about mummies speaking, gave Rosie a delicious shivery feeling. Outside, the maple tree rustled in the breeze, and the sparkles on Winky's mummy shimmered in the moonlight, as though promising bright things to come—not eternal life, but eternal fame for Winky Blue.

Yummy Mummy!

"I can't believe we're finally here!" said Eliza, as the school bus pulled up across the street from the museum. A truck had broken down on the turnpike, and the bus had stood still in traffic for what seemed like forever.

"When are we going to get to the museum?" Gina had kept asking. "My cat mummy can't wait forever to win a prize."

"Mummies are very patient," Mrs. Kompass reminded her with a smile. "Some of them waited thousands of years to be discovered."

"I don't want to wait a thousand years for Kiddles's mummy to be discovered," grumped Gina.

"Meow!" added Kiddles, from her cat carrier.

"By the time this bus gets to New York, we'll all be mummies!" predicted Olivia.

Now Rosie peered across the street at the massive gray building that spanned several city blocks.

"The American Museum of Natural History," she said softly. It looked like a castle or a fortress with its tall towers and stately stone pillars.

"History, mystery!" prattled Winky Blue, from his travel cage.

"Ha!" thought Rosie. "The only mystery is whose mummy is going to win first prize today. And I already know the answer to that!"

Everyone was talking excitedly.

"Olivia sat on my frog mummy!" cried Travis.

"At least she didn't sit on your frog," said Eliza.

"Ribbit! Ribbit!" agreed Gleep, Travis's frog.

"I'm starving!" moaned Jonathan. "When are we going to eat?"

"Yummy mummy!" said Winky Blue, poking his head through the bars of his cage and pecking a sparkle off his mummy.

"Winky, stop that!" scolded Rosie.

"Class, quiet please!" called Mrs. Kompass. "Remember the rules. Dogs are not allowed beyond the lobby, and all pets must be on a leash or in a cage or container."

"Not mine!" said Kelli, hugging her stuffed Tyrannosaurus. Children who didn't own live pets had been allowed to bring stuffed ones so they wouldn't feel left out. Kelli was the only one with a dinosaur mummy.

"Do you all have your mummies?" asked Mrs. Kompass.

"I have my mummy and my mommy," answered Travis. Everyone laughed. Travis's mother had come along on the trip. So had Rosie's Aunt Maria.

"Everyone stay together as we enter the museum," Mrs. Kompass reminded the class.

Rosie gripped Winky's cage tightly as she hurried across the street with Aunt Maria. A moment later, they were sweeping through the revolving doors and into the immense museum. A gigantic dinosaur skeleton towered majestically over the lobby. Michael, Rosie, and Eliza stared in awe at its long neck and tiny head arching high up toward the vaulted ceiling. Raffles growled.

"I wouldn't want to meet that dinosaur in a dark alley," said Eliza.

Mrs. Kompass laughed. "It would have to be a pretty big alley for a Barosaurus to fit into."

Winky Blue cocked his head and peered curiously at the monstrous skeleton. "And the children say he could laugh and play just the same as you and me!" he sang. Winky had learned all the songs on Rosie's holiday sing-along tape by heart, and goodness knows he liked showing off—especially when there was a crowd.

Rosie laughed. "Winky is really interested in that Baro—whatever it's called."

"Maybe that's because dinosaurs are related to birds," Michael said. He loved animals of all kinds and knew a lot about them. "I read that birds are actually modern-day dinosaurs."

"That means that Winky Blue is a living dinosaur," marvelled Rosie.

"A Wink-a-saurus," said Eliza, with a laugh.

Michael nodded. "Maybe one day, about 150

million years from now, kids will stand right here looking at Winky's skeleton."

"I'd rather they looked at Winky the way he is, alive and covered with feathers," said Rosie, who didn't like thinking about Winky's skeleton without his body wrapped around it.

"Right on!" crowed Winky Blue. "Hurrah for the pumpkin pie!"

Two more school buses pulled up, and soon the lobby was teeming with excited kids, meowing cats, curious gerbils, and pet mummies of all shapes and sizes.

"Attention, please!" announced a man in a white lab coat. "My name is Dr. Ramos. Will everyone please line up to register with the judges? The pet mummy contest will begin in twenty minutes!"

"I wonder if he's a mummy doctor," said Rosie.

"Raffles's mummy is going to need a doctor if its tail keeps falling off," grumbled Eliza.

Behind Dr. Ramos, at a long table, sat the judging panel—a group of very serious looking people.

"They must be the judges," said Gina.

Rosie surveyed the other pet mummies. There were snail mummies, mouse mummies, frog mummies, fish mummies, bunny mummies, and even a monkey mummy.

Michael nudged Rosie. "Look," he said, pointing to a tall red-haired girl, standing in line ahead of them. She was holding a birdcage with a canary in it. On the door of the cage, in large gold letters, was the name Goldie.

Michael waved to the canary. "Hi, Goldie!"

The canary fluffed her feathers, looking pleased with herself. Rosie could see why. Goldie's canary mummy was covered with hundreds of glittering diamonds and emeralds. Well, they were probably only glass beads, thought Rosie, but they glittered like real jewels. And that wasn't all. Under her arm, the red-haired girl

held a canary-sized Egyptian pyramid.

"Goldie must be a canary queen to have a whole pyramid all her own," Michael whispered to Rosie.

"But we were only supposed to make mummies, not mummy habitats," Rosie whispered back, kicking herself for not thinking of the idea on her own.

Aunt Maria noticed her worried look. "Don't worry," she said, squeezing Rosie's hand. "You worked hard on your mummy, and that's what really matters."

Rosie didn't say anything, but she wasn't so sure.

What really mattered to Rosie was winning a place for Winky Blue in a real museum.

Hall of
North
American
Mammals

Chocolate Footprints

Rosie watched as the red-haired girl stepped up to the judging platform. All four judges leaned forward and gazed admiringly at the dazzling canary mummy.

"You have a magnificent mummy there!" one judge remarked.

"And a marvelous pyramid," added another.

Winky leaned out and pecked another sparkle off his mummy.

"Winky, stop it!" hissed Rosie. With competition like Goldie, Winky's mummy needed every sparkle it had!

"Naughty boy!" retorted Winky, and he pecked off two more sparkles.

Rosie and Eliza registered their pet mummies with the judges. Michael stepped up next.

"And who is this?" asked a judge, smiling at Cinnamon.

"Cinnamon," Michael replied. "He's a gerbil, but Mr. Blackwell at the pet store says there's a rumor that his great-great-great-grandfather was a pack rat."

"A pack rat?" asked the judge, looking startled and not at all sure she wanted to be near such a creature.

Michael nodded. "He's super-friendly," he assured the judge. "He'll even nibble your ears. See?" Michael lifted Cinnamon out of his cage and thrust him toward the judge. Surprised, the judge jumped back, knocking over her chair. The chair fell with a bang, startling Cinnamon who leapt out of Michael's hands and scurried away. Michael went chasing after him.

"Cinnamon, come back!" Michael called frantically.

Excited, Raffles joined in the chase, pulling Eliza along behind him.

"Rosie, help!" cried Eliza, tugging on Raffles's leash. "I can't hold him!"

Rosie ran after Eliza, holding Winky's cage and his mummy in one hand while trying to grab hold of Raffles's leash with the other.

Michael raced ahead of them.

"Cinnamon, slow down!" Michael shouted.

Instead of slowing down, Cinnamon picked up speed. He raced down two flights of stairs and around a corner into the Big Dipper Ice Cream Cafe, with Raffles close behind.

"I never realized Raffles was so strong!" panted Eliza, hanging on to Raffles's leash for dear life. Rosie was still trying to get hold of it.

In the ice cream cafe, Cinnamon scampered under tables and around chairs. A little boy was walking to one of the tables, balancing a tray in his hands. Cinnamon scurried between his feet. The boy yelled and dropped his Big

Bang Ice Cream Sundae. Ice cream, sprinkles, and chocolate syrup splattered everywhere. Cinnamon slid through the sticky syrup, leaving a trail of chocolate footprints as he dashed out of the lunchroom and up the stairway on the other side, with Raffles still close behind.

"Thumpity-thump-thump, thumpity-thump-thump look at Frosty go!" sang Winky Blue.

"Raffles, you're going to be so grounded for this!" cried Eliza. "And no Doggie Donuts for a month!"

Upstairs, Cinnamon darted into the Hall of North American Mammals. When Michael tried to follow him, a security guard blocked him at the door.

"Stop!" the security guard ordered.

Michael stopped so suddenly that Rosie and Eliza bumped into him. Raffles stopped, too, finally. He sat down, panting.

"This hall is closed," said the guard. A newspaper, *The New York Comet*, is here photographing one of the Western wildlife scenes."

"But Cinnamon—" began Michael.

"I'm sorry," interrupted the guard, "but we have to remove the glass from the display cases in order to take photographs, and absolutely no one is allowed in the Hall of North American Mammals until they're finished."

"Can't we take Raffles in?" pleaded Michael. "He's a North American mammal."

"Woof!" added Raffles, as if to prove it.

"That North American mammal is going to get you into big trouble if you don't get him out of here right now," warned the guard, pointing to Raffles. Then he closed the heavy doors to the hall and disappeared inside.

Eliza sighed. "I guess I'd better take Raffles back to the lobby. Raffles, heel!" she commanded.

But instead of heeling, Raffles wriggled out of his collar and bounded off in another direction.

"He must be going around another way to

catch up with Cinnamon," said Michael.

"Raffles isn't really that smart," Eliza pointed out.

"Well, his nose is!" said Michael. "Let's go!"

Raffles led them into a dim room filled with ancient human skulls and models of hairy cave dwellers crouched inside glass display cases.

Raffles stopped directly under the nose of Neanderthal man. He put his tail between his legs and whimpered.

"He's lost the scent," whispered Eliza. It seemed right to whisper in the dim room filled with ancient skeletons and secrets of the past.

"You mean he's lost his nerve," said Michael. "He's probably afraid of Neanderthal man."

"It is kind of spooky in here," whispered Rosie.

"Spooks, kooks!" exclaimed Winky in a loud voice. Everyone laughed and the dim hall seemed less forbidding.

Michael paused to study a map of the museum.

"The rooms are laid out in a big circle," he pointed out. "If we go around through the Hall of Gems, we might get lucky and meet Cinnamon coming the other way."

Michael was right about Cinnamon's escape route. But he hadn't counted on his speed. Even before they could enter the Hall of Gems, Cinnamon came racing out. Chasing after him was a security guard.

"Stop that thief!" he yelled. "He stole the White Orient Pearl!"

Mummy Mess

Rosie watched in disbelief as Cinnamon streaked by. In his mouth she caught the gleam of something shiny and white.

"Don't let him escape!" shouted the guard. "That pearl is worth millions!"

Michael tried to grab Cinnamon as he darted under a life-size Native American canoe, but he came up empty-handed. Cinnamon raced on, past Native American baskets and colorful headdresses. By now three more guards and several other official-looking people had joined the chase. Cinnamon bolted past a tall totem pole and into the passageway beyond.

"O'er the fields we go—laughing all the way!" sang Winky. But no one was laughing. Cinnamon had vanished—again.

"Secure the museum. Cover all entrances and exits!" ordered a woman who seemed to be in charge. Rosie noticed she wore a badge that read, "Dr. Karin Greene, Head Curator."

A moment later a voice boomed over the public-address system:

"Attention! The White Orient Pearl has been stolen. All museum exits and entrances will be temporarily closed to keep the thief from escaping!"

"Cinnamon isn't a thief," cried Michael. "He's my gerbil, and he's never stolen anything in his life. . .er. . .except for food, that is. . . ."

Dr. Greene looked at Michael with surprise. "That's odd," she said. "He is behaving more like a pack rat than a gerbil."

Michael said nothing. But he remembered the rumor about Cinnamon's great-great-great-grand father being a pack rat. Maybe Cinnamon's pack rat past was catching up with him!

"We are always so careful to guard the gems when we remove them from the display cases for lectures," said Dr. Greene. "But that gerbil was fast! I turned my back for one second after opening the case and he zoomed in, grabbed the pearl, and was off!"

"I, Harvey Higgins, have been curator of the jewels and gems for twenty-five years and not one has ever been stolen!" declared one of the men with Dr. Greene. "And now a rat has absconded with the pearl that once graced the crown of Queen Elizabeth I!"

"Way to go!" cheered Winky Blue. Mr. Higgins glared at him.

Just then a second announcement came over the public-address system.

"Rosie Linares, Michael Humphrey, and Eliza Collins, please return to the lobby immediately."

"The mummy contest must be starting," said Rosie. "We'd better get back to the lobby."

"Don't go too far," Dr. Greene warned Michael. "We may need to talk to you."

In the lobby, guards were posted at the doors to make sure no visitors came in or went out of the museum.

Aunt Maria hurried up to Rosie. "Thank goodness you're back! There's a dangerous thief loose in the museum!"

"Cinnamon is not dangerous!" said Michael.

"Cinnamon!" exclaimed Mrs. Kompass. "What in the world are you talking about, Michael?"

"Cinnamon spice and everything nice!" chattered Winky.

"Now, Winky, let us tell the story," said Rosie. But before she could begin, Dr. Ramos made an announcement.

"The pet mummy contest is now underway!"

The butterflies in Rosie's stomach started doing loops and circles. This was the moment she had been waiting for!

Rosie took a deep breath and placed her parakeet mummy on the display table. Winky had pecked off most of the sparkles, she noticed, and one wing had been broken when Rosie had collided with Michael and Eliza outside the Hall of North American Mammals. To top it off, the mummy was splattered with chocolate syrup from the Big Bang Ice Cream Sundae debacle.

Rosie looked at the brilliant array of pet mummies on the table, and her heart sank. Winky Blue's mummy was a mess! And not even a mummy doctor could fix it.

Wink-a-saurus

Goldie the canary won first prize in the pet mummy contest. The monkey mummy won second, and Travis's mummy frog won third.

Mrs. Kompass congratulated him. "Good going, Travis. And you, too, Gleep!"

Rosie wanted to feel happy for Travis and Gleep, but it was hard when she was feeling so bad about Winky Blue.

"Poor mummy!" said Winky, pecking off the last mummy sparkle.

"Winky's future is ruined—and it's all thanks to Cinnamon!" cried Rosie. "If he hadn't run away, Raffles wouldn't have run after him, and we wouldn't have had to run after Raffles, and Winky's mummy would still be all bright and beautiful."

"Don't blame Cinnamon," said Michael. "He didn't mean to cause trouble—and now he's lost!"

"Cinnamon's a loser, and that's all he is," said Rosie.

Michael looked as if he'd been slapped. Even Eliza looked shocked. Rosie felt bad about what she'd said—but not bad enough to take it back. After all, Michael had never really cared about whether his gerbil mummy won a prize, while Rosie had such high hopes for her sparkly parakeet mummy!

Detectives and police continued to search the huge, cavernous museum for the missing pearl. Their walkie-talkies crackled and buzzed as they talked back and forth.

While they waited, Michael told Mrs. Kompass and the class all about what had happened. He talked fast and didn't look at Rosie once.

Rosie felt awful about Winky losing the contest, but now she began to feel even worse about calling Cinnamon a loser and hurting Michael's feelings. It was true Michael didn't have dreams of fame and stardom for Cinnamon, but that's one reason he was such a good friend. He always stood firmly behind Rosie, celebrating with her when Winky did something heroic and helping when he was lost or in trouble. And now Cinnamon was the one who was lost—maybe forever.

Just as Rosie was wondering if she'd ever see Cinnamon again, the little gerbil appeared at Michael's feet, as if by magic.

Michael scooped his pet up joyfully. "Cinnamon, you came back!"

"Tell the police! Cinnamon has given himself up!" yelled Travis.

A team of detectives and guards, headed

by Dr. Greene hurried over. While everyone watched, Dr. Greene gently pried open Cinnamon's jaws and peered into his mouth. Then she gasped.

"The pearl is gone!"

"Maybe he swallowed it," suggested Eliza.

"Or hid it," said Gina.

"That rat is nothing but a thief," muttered Mr. Higgins.

Rosie decided to speak up. "Cinnamon is not a rat or a thief," she countered. "He's a lovable gerbil."

Michael looked at Rosie gratefully. He understood that Rosie was sorry for what she'd said about Cinnamon.

"There's a story that Cinnamon's great-great-great-grandfather was a pack rat, and pack rats have a habit of taking shiny objects and hiding them in secret places," Michael explained.

"That is a bad habit!" retorted Mr. Higgins.

"Now everyone stay calm," said Dr. Greene.

"We'll find the pearl. We must. It is on loan to the museum and it is irreplaceable!"

All at once, an idea flashed into Rosie's mind. Her face lit up. "My parakeet Winky Blue might be able to help find the pearl," she said to Dr. Greene. "He's good at spotting shiny objects."

"Winky Blue is really heroic," Michael chimed in. "He found a gold key once that helped save Cinnamon's life."

Dr. Greene looked doubtful.

"I just know Winky could help," said Rosie. "Right, Winky Blue?"

Rosie looked down at Winky—but he wasn't there. Wink-a-saurus, the feathered dinosaur, was gone.

Winky Blue Goes Wild

"Winky's gone!" cried Rosie. "He was here just a minute ago. Now his cage door is open, and he's disappeared!"

Michael stared at the cage. "That's impossible. I tied the door closed with a secret Boy Scout knot that's absolutely foolproof."

"Well, Winky's no fool," Rosie declared. "He must have figured out how to untie it. Now he's gone!"

Aunt Maria covered her eyes. "I think I'm having déjà vu."

"What kind of you?" asked Eliza.

"Déjà vu," repeated Aunt Maria, "a feeling that something has happened before."

"This has happened before!" said Rosie. "And each time I promise myself it will never happen again!"

"Now, Rosie, stay calm," said Aunt Maria, sounding like Dr. Greene. "We won't leave the museum until we find Winky."

Rosie thought of the enormous museum with its endless passages, stairways, and great halls. Finding Winky would be even harder than finding a runaway gerbil—or a hidden pearl.

Rosie swallowed hard. This day was not turning out the way she had expected. Her dreams of eternal fame for Winky Blue were spoiled. His mummy was a major mess. And worst of all, Winky Blue himself had vanished.

"Come on, Rosie," said Aunt Maria. "Let's go look for Winky."

"Cinnamon and I will come along to help," offered Michael.

Just as they were leaving, Rosie noticed a quotation inscribed on the wall in large letters:

"*There* are no words that can tell
the hidden spirit of the wilderness,
that can reveal its mystery—"
Theodore Roosevelt

I hope I can reveal the mystery of what's happened to Winky Blue! thought Rosie, as she walked off with Michael and Aunt Maria. Eliza had to stay in the lobby with Raffles.

While the police searched the museum for the royal pearl, Rosie, Michael, and Aunt Maria searched for Winky Blue. They looked in the Hall of Gems, where they gazed at rings and necklaces encrusted with dazzling jewels. They searched Birds of the World and the Hall of Ocean Life. They saw many marvelous sights, but no sign of Winky Blue.

"Here, Winky. Where are you, Winky Blue?" called Rosie. But the only birds she saw were the stuffed ones in the display cases.

Upstairs and downstairs they went, through great rooms and long hallways, past the ancient human skulls and Neanderthal man. They followed a trail of giant claw prints painted on the floor, but they only led to the school lunchroom where Rosie's class was eating their brown bag lunches.

Michael looked thoughtful. "Maybe Winky got sucked into a time warp and evolved back into a dinosaur," he said, as they trudged back up the stairs.

"Or maybe he revolved—right out of the revolving front door!" said Rosie. "He could be lost in New York City!"

Though the museum was sealed off, police and detectives had continued going in and out through the revolving doors, organizing the search.

The New York Comet had finished photographing, and the Hall of North American Mammals was open again. Rosie, Michael, and

Aunt Maria walked through, past display cases where stuffed bison grazed on broad prairies, looking eerily lifelike with the Western sunset blazing behind them.

"Winky, where are you?" called Rosie.

A kindergarten class stood looking at the display of a bison herd grazing on the grassy plains of Montana.

"I didn't know they had wild parakeets out west," said a teacher.

"It's a living one, too!" said a boy standing beside her.

"Way to go!" cried a familiar voice.

Rosie ran up to the display case. There, perched on top of a bison's head, was Winky Blue!

"Winky!" cried Rosie. "How on Earth did you get in there?"

Michael stared at Winky in amazement. "He must have flown in there when the newspaper people took the glass out of the display case," he reasoned.

Winky looked up and spotted Rosie. "Right on, Rosie!" he cried.

Rosie couldn't believe it. Winky Blue was in the Wild West—right in the middle of New York City!

"Oh, dear!" said Aunt Maria. "Winky does manage to get himself into some interesting mischief."

Winky seemed unconcerned.

"Hello! Wipe your feet. Do your homework!" he chatted, hopping down into a prairie dog hole.

"Isn't he cute?" said a spiky-haired little boy.

"He's smart, too. Hello, birdie!" said a girl with pigtails, tapping against the glass.

"Do your homework! Frosty's coming to town!" chattered Winky, who was enjoying the attention.

The kindergartners laughed, but Rosie didn't think it was funny.

"Aunt Maria, we have to get Winky out of

that case!" she cried. "He'll die trapped in there without food or water."

"There's someone over there who may be able to help us," said Aunt Maria, pointing to a security guard standing across the room.

Rosie hurried over to the guard.

"Please come and help!" Rosie pleaded. "I've got to get that display case opened right away!"

"I'm afraid that's impossible," said the guard. "We only open the display cases for very special occasions."

"But this is a special occasion. I have to get that bird!" cried Rosie, pointing at Winky.

The guard shook his head. "All birds and animals in the display cases belong to the museum. Not a single one can be removed!"

Trapped!

"But you don't understand! Winky Blue doesn't belong to the museum," Rosie explained. "He belongs to me."

"He can't stay in the glass case without food or water, or he'll become extinct like that Barosaurus," added Michael. "This is urgent!"

The guard made a call on his radio and soon Dr. Greene appeared with her assistants. They, too, stared in astonishment at Winky Blue inside the display case.

"That's my niece's parakeet," Aunt Maria informed them. "He must have flown in there when the reporter from the newspaper was taking photographs."

"He's not stuffed, either!" piped up the spiky-haired kindergarten boy.

"He was made of snow but the children know how he came to life that day!" sang Winky Blue, poking his head out of the prairie dog hole. The kindergartners howled with delight.

"No, he certainly isn't stuffed," said Dr. Greene. "I'll arrange to get the display case opened right away."

"Don't worry Winky—we're going to rescue you!" called Rosie through the glass.

"Oh, my! Hurrah for the pumpkin pie!" replied Winky. The kindergartners shrieked.

A few minutes later Dr. Greene came back with two museum workers.

"I've been working here almost all my life," said one of the workers, shaking his head, "and I've never seen anything like this."

"It has been quite a day," said Dr. Greene. "First a gerbil runs off with a famous crown

jewel, and then a parakeet flies inside one of our display cases!"

Dr. Greene cleared the room, except for Rosie, Michael, and Aunt Maria. They stood by as the workers carefully opened the display case. But even then, Winky refused to come out of the prairie dog hole.

"Winky likes it out west," offered Michael.

"Winky Blue, you come out of there right now!" ordered Rosie.

Winky poked his head out of the prairie dog hole and blinked at Rosie. Then he dived back in.

"Right on!" Winky Blue said in a muffled voice.

Dr. Greene leaned over, lifted Winky out, and gently handed him to Rosie.

"Oh, Winky, I'm so glad to see you!" said Rosie with relief. "I don't care if your mummy didn't win a prize. I'd rather have you alive right now than famous forever."

Winky said nothing. He couldn't say anything because he was holding something in his beak— something white and round and shiny.

The White Orient Pearl.

The Greatest Rock Group Ever

"Well, I'll be," said Dr. Greene. "I'LL BE!"

"Wow, Winky Blue!" cried Rosie. "You found the pearl!"

"Way to go!" said Winky Blue as the pearl dropped out of his beak and into Dr. Greene's hands.

"Winky, you're a superhero!" said Rosie.

"I think I need to sit down," said Aunt Maria.

News that Winky Blue had found Queen Elizabeth's pearl quickly spread through the museum. Police and detectives abandoned their search, Rosie's class cheered, and *The New York Comet* came back to cover the story. Rosie and Michael told the reporters all about how Winky Blue had recovered the missing pearl.

"And it's all thanks to Cinnamon!" finished Rosie, smiling at Michael. "If Cinnamon hadn't hidden the pearl in the prairie dog hole, Winky never would have found it."

Dr. Greene nodded. "Cinnamon must have been attracted to the Western wildlife scene," she explained. "After all, a pack rat's natural habitat is out west."

"And a pack rat's natural hiding place is a prairie dog hole," added Mrs. Kompass.

Aunt Maria looked puzzled. "What I want to know is how Winky managed to find the pearl after Cinnamon hid it?"

Everyone had a different theory about that. Travis was sure that Winky had noticed a gleam of light reflecting off the pearl. Jonathan thought that maybe Winky was attracted to the wildlife scene and had stumbled upon the pearl by accident. Rosie insisted that Winky Blue was quite simply a genius and could find anything.

Photographers snapped pictures, and reporters scribbled notes. Then the museum gave Rosie's whole class free ice cream sundaes at the Big Dipper Ice Cream Cafe. Afterward, everyone packed up their pets and pet mummies, and Michael tied Winky's cage door closed with a double secret Boy Scout knot.

"No one, not even Houdini, the great magician, could untie this!" Michael vowed.

Before they boarded the school bus, Dr. Greene presented Rosie with a small brown envelope. "This is for you and Winky Blue, for outstanding detective work," she announced.

"Thank you," said Rosie, feeling awed and proud.

"Hurry and open it!" begged Eliza as the school bus pulled away from the curb.

Pretty soon everyone started guessing what was inside the envelope.

"Maybe it's a million dollars!"

"Or a gold medal!"

"Or a dinosaur bone."

Rosie tore open the envelope. She stared.

"Tell us what it is!" demanded Olivia.

"Is it a million dollars?" asked Michael, trying to peer over Rosie's shoulder.

"No," Rosie smiled, "it's tickets for three to go see a big rock group."

"No way!" said Winky. Winky Blue hated rock music and refused to sing along when Rosie's favorite group played on the radio. Aunt Maria said he had good taste.

"Do they play any songs I know?" asked Travis, looking interested.

"Are they famous?" asked Olivia.

"Is it that new group, Cookies and Cream?" Gina wanted to know.

Rosie smiled. "It's the greatest rock group ever," she said, as she handed the envelope to Aunt Maria.

"Why Rosie," exclaimed Aunt Maria, "these are airplane tickets! We are going to see the Mount Rushmore National Monument in South Dakota!"

"What's that got to do with rock groups?" asked Jonathan.

"I know!" Michael burst out. "Four presidents carved in rock!"

"That's right!" said Mrs. Kompass, "They are indeed the greatest rock group ever!"

Rosie's class had seen photographs of the four famous presidents carved into a mountainside—George Washington, Abraham Lincoln,

Thomas Jefferson, and Theodore Roosevelt.

Theodore Roosevelt! Rosie remembered the words she had read on the museum wall that morning. It seemed like a long time ago now.

"There are no words that can tell

the hidden spirit of the wilderness,

that can reveal its mystery—"

Winky hadn't revealed the hidden spirit of the wilderness, but he had solved the mystery of the missing pearl.

"Now Winky Blue will get a chance to see the real Wild West," said Aunt Maria.

"Hooray for Winky Blue!" cheered Rosie.

"Winky Blue, buckle your shoe!" chirped Winky.

All the kids were laughing and chatting as the bus inched slowly through the heavy traffic. But Rosie didn't hear them, and she hardly noticed the bustling city around her. She was thinking about Mount Rushmore. In her mind, she saw the majestic monument with the four

famous presidents looking out with stony, serene faces. And right next to them, carved into the rock, was a giant replica of Winky Blue.

"Hello! Rosie?" said Michael, nudging her. "Did you hear what I said? We're about to go through the tunnel."

"I think Winky Blue would make a great president, don't you?" murmured Rosie dreamily.

"No way!" said Winky Blue. "Right on!"

Michael laughed. "Sure. You'd never have to guess what he was thinking."

"And he'd give very short speeches," Eliza added from the seat behind.

The bus rumbled through the Lincoln Tunnel. Dusk was falling as the bus left the tunnel and reentered New Jersey. Across the Hudson River, Rosie could see the lights of Manhattan mirrored in the dark waters. The future glimmered before her—a distant and wonderful dream. Perhaps the trip to Mount Rushmore would be the shining peak of Winky's career (even if he didn't become president). That was fun to think about. But for now—for just this one moment—it was enough that Winky Blue was back with Rosie, right where he belonged.